WALT DISNEY'S

DUMBO

ILLUSTRATED BY THE WALT DISNEY STUDIO

GOLDEN PRESS
Western Publishing Company, Inc.
Racine, Wisconsin

This Little Golden Book was produced under the supervision of

THE WALT DISNEY STUDIO

WALT DISNEY BOOKS

Little Golden Books here bring you, in gay color, delightful stories and illustrations adapted from the world-famous Walt Disney Motion Pictures. In them you will find Pinocchio, The Three Little Pigs, Bambi, Dumbo, Uncle Remus, Cinderella, Alice in Wonderland, Peter Pan, and many other well-loved Disney characters.

I T was spring—spring in the circus! Everyone was singing. Everyone was happy.

Happiest of all was Mrs. Jumbo, for in her stall in the circus train was a chubby, brand-new baby elephant. Though the other animals called the baby Dumbo, his mother loved him dearly. Even though his ears *were* big.

"All aboard!" shouted the ringmaster.

After a long winter's rest, it was time to set out again on the open road.

"Toot! Toot!" whistled Casey Jones, the locomotive of the circus train.

And with a jiggety jerk and a brisk puff-puff, off sped Casey Jones!

It was dark when Casey Jones whistled and puffed into the station. Rain poured down hard, but the circus began to unload. The workmen jumped down from the freight cars.

They lighted torches and stuck them in the ground. Men and animals came bustling out of the train into the windy, wet night. They all helped to get the circus tent up—even Mrs. Jumbo's new baby helped.

By morning the rain had stopped, the tent was all set up, and the circus was busy getting ready for the big parade. The band played. Everyone fell in line.

Then off pranced the gay procession down the main street. There were creamy-white horses, licorice-colored seals! There were lady acrobats in pink silk tights, lions pacing in their gilded wagon-cages, elephants marching with slow, even steps.

The crowds on the sidewalk cheered. Then, suddenly, their eyes opened wide. They craned their necks. "Look . . . look!" they cried. "Look at that silly animal with the draggy ears! He can't be an elephant

. . . he must be a clown!" They burst out in loud laughs.

Sadly, Dumbo toddled behind his mother, with his trunk clasped to her tail. He tried to hurry along faster so he wouldn't hear the laughter, but he stumbled. He tripped over his ears. Down he splashed into a puddle of mud. Now the crowds laughed even louder. Mrs. Jumbo scowled at them. She picked Dumbo up and carried him in her trunk the rest of the way.

When the parade finally came back to the tent, Mrs. Jumbo put Dumbo in her wooden bathtub, and as she scrubbed she whispered comforting words.

A gang of noisy boys came pushing in first for the

afternoon show. "We want to see the elephant," they yelled, "—the one with the sailboat ears!" "Look . . . there he is."

A boy grabbed one of Dumbo's ears and pulled it hard. Then he made an ugly face and stuck out his tongue.

Mrs. Jumbo couldn't stand it. She snatched the boy up with her trunk, dropped him across the rope, and spanked him, hard.

"Help!" he cried, "Help! Help!"

"What's going on here?" cried the ringmaster and snapped his whip at Mrs. Jumbo. "Tie her down!" he yelled.

Mrs. Jumbo reared on her hind legs. But soon she was behind the bars in the prison wagon with a big sign that said: "Danger! Mad Elephant! Keep Out!"

The next day, they made Dumbo into a clown. They painted his face with a foolish grin and dressed him in a baby dress. On his head they put a bonnet. They used him in the most ridiculous act in the show—a make-believe fire. He had to jump from the top of a blazing cardboard house, down into a firemen's net. The audience thought it a great joke. But Dumbo felt disgraced.

"He's a disgrace to us," the big animals agreed, and turned their backs on him.

Hidden in a pile of hay was Timothy Mouse, the smallest animal with the circus.

"They can't treat the little fellow that way," he muttered. "Not while Timothy Mouse is around."

"Hey there, little fellow!" he called to Dumbo. "Don't be afraid. I'm your friend. I want to help you."

"Say!" he went on, staring at Dumbo's ears. "Those ears are as good as wings. I'll teach you to fly!"

Quietly Dumbo and Timothy crept out of the tent to Mother Jumbo.

Dumbo told her all about the clown act, and how unhappy he was without her and about the wonderful idea Timothy had for making him a success.

Then sadly they said good-night, and Timothy and Dumbo continued on their way.

With Timothy as teacher Dumbo practiced running and jumping and hopping. He tried slow and fast takeoffs and standing and running jumps. He stretched out his wings and flapped them, 1-2-3-4. Then he tried the whole thing together. But hard as he tried, Dumbo could not leave the ground.

At last, almost too tired to stand, the two friends gave up and started gloomily back toward the sleeping circus.

"Don't worry, Dumbo," Timothy whispered as he curled up on Dumbo's hat brim for a good night's sleep. "We'll have you flying yet!"

When the morning sun arose, Timothy was the first to awaken. He blinked and looked up. Just above him, four old black crows sat and stared at him.

"Why . . . why . . ." yawned Timothy, rubbing his eyes. "Where am I?"

"You're up in our tree," snapped the crows crossly. "That's where you are."

"Tree?" gasped Timothy. He looked around. Sure enough, there he was, sitting on a branch. He and Dumbo were up in a tree! The ground was far, far below. "But . . . but . . . how did we get here?" he stammered.

"How!" cackled the crows. "You and that elephant just came a-flyin' up!"

"Flying!" Timothy yelled. "Dumbo, Dumbo, wake up! Dumbo, we're up in a tree! You FLEW here!"

Slowly Dumbo opened his eyes. He glanced down. He gulped. Then he struggled to his feet. But suddenly he slipped on the smooth tree bark and fell. Down . . . down . . . down! He bounced from branch to branch, with Timothy clinging to his trunk. Plonk! They landed in a shallow pond just underneath the tree. The crows chuckled and cawed from above.

Timothy scrambled up out of the water and wrung out Dumbo's tail. "Dumbo," he panted. "You can fly! If you can fly when you're asleep, you can fly when

you're awake. Your ears, Dumbo, they're your fortune!"
He grabbed one of Dumbo's wet ears and patted it.
"You won't be a clown any more. You'll be famous
. . . the only flying elephant in the whole wide world!"

And Timothy and Dumbo began all over again to
practice flying.

But it wasn't easy. Time after time, Dumbo tried to
take off. Time after time, he sprawled out flat on his
face. Soon the crows began to feel sorry for the little
fellow. When Timothy told them all the sad things
that had happened to Dumbo because of his big ears,
they flew down and offered to help.

One of the crows took Timothy aside. "Flying's just
like swimming," he whispered. "It's just a matter of

believing that you can do it." He turned and snatched a long, black feather from his tail.

"Here, take this . . . tell the baby elephant it's a magic feather. Tell him if he holds it, he can fly." The boss crow winked and flew off.

Timothy handed Dumbo the feather and scurried up his trunk to the brim of his cap. He held his breath!

The trick worked like a charm. The very instant that Dumbo wrapped the tip of his trunk around the feather, flap . . . flap . . . flap! went his ears. Up into the air he soared like a bird! Over the tallest treetops he sailed. He glided, he dipped, he dived. Three times he circled over the heads of cheering crows. Then he headed back to the circus grounds.

Timothy shouted, "We must keep your flying a secret—a surprise for your act in this afternoon's show."

No one noticed Dumbo when he and Timothy came quietly back. It was already time for Dumbo to get into his costume. Inside the walls of a cardboard house he had to wait all through the show until fire crackled up around him.

At last Timothy leaned down and handed him the feather.

Cr..rr..rr..ack! Cr..rr..ack! crackled the fire. The clown act was on! Flames shot up around the cardboard house. Clang! Clang! roared the clown fire-engine, rushing toward the blaze.

From the far end of the ring, a red-headed mother clown came running. "Save my baby!" she screamed. "He's on the top floor!"

The firemen brought a big net and held it out.

"Jump, my darling baby, jump!" shrieked the mother clown.

Dumbo jumped, but as he jumped the black feather slipped from his trunk and floated away. Now his magic was gone, and Dumbo plunged down like a stone.

Timothy saw the feather go. "The feather's a fake," he shouted frantically to Dumbo. "You can fly!"

Dumbo heard the shout and, doubtfully, spread his ears wide. Not two feet above the net he stopped his plunge and swooped up into the air!

A mighty gasp arose from the audience. They knew it couldn't be, but it was! Dumbo was flying!

While the crowd roared its delight, Dumbo did power dives, loops, spins, and barrel rolls. He swooped down to pick up peanuts and squirted a trunkful of water on the clowns.

The keepers freed Mrs. Jumbo and brought her to the tent in triumph to see her baby fly. So all of Dumbo's worries had come to an end.

By evening, Dumbo was a hero from coast to coast.

Timothy became his manager, and saw to it that Dumbo got a wonderful contract with a big salary and a pension for his mother.

The circus was renamed "Dumbo's Flying Circus."

And Dumbo traveled in a special streamlined car.
But best of all, he forgave everyone who had been
unkind to him, for his heart was as big as his ears.